THE REINCARNATION

SURYANSH SACHAN

Made with ♥ on the Notion Press Platform
www.notionpress.com

To the pillars of my life ---

Mummy, *Swechchha Sachan* — whose love is the first story I ever knew.
Papa, *Rahul Sachan* — whose strength taught me how to stand tall.
And to my little brother, **Manas** —
whose innocence reminds me of the world we need to protect.

This story belongs to you.

Contents

Preface

This story was not written for entertainment alone — it was written from anger, grief, and a desperate hope.

I was deeply shaken by the horrors of the **Nirbhaya Case** and the incident at **RG Kar Medical College**, among countless others that go unnoticed. These were not just events — they were brutal reminders of a world where safety is still a privilege, not a right, for women.

The Reincarnation was born from the desire to imagine a world where justice doesn't fail, where silence doesn't win, and where no woman ever has to be afraid again.

Through the voice of Sati, reborn as Shiv, I've tried to channel that longing for justice — not only in the courts, but in the soul of society.

If this story moves you, shakes you, or changes something in you — even the smallest thing — then it has done its job.

— *Suryansh Sachan*

Acknowledgements

To my **Mummy**, *Swechchha Sachan*, and **Papa**, *Rahul Sachan* — thank you for being the roots I always return to, the ones who believed in me even before I believed in myself.

To my little brother *Manas,* whose innocence and constant chatter remind me what pure joy looks like.

To **Amul Mishra (Aryamitra)** — my partner in chaos, creativity, and courage. Your presence in my life is nothing short of magic.

To **DCAC**, the college that shaped my voice and gave me the courage to share it with the world.

To **every woman and girl — this story is for you. For your fire, your pain, your fight, and your dignity. You are the reason this story exists. You are the reason it must be told.**

And yes, to ChatGPT — my creative storming companion, who brought rhythm to the noise and helped me carve meaning from the madness.

Prologue

"They thought they buried me that night.
But the soil does not swallow rage.
It remembers.
And it returns."

The wind that night carried no song—only silence.

In a village forgotten by time, beneath the indifferent sky, a girl's screams vanished into darkness. Sati's body lay broken, but her soul did not rest. Her blood sank into the earth, not as surrender—but as a promise.

The gods watched. The stars turned away. The law slept.

But something ancient awakened.

For when justice is denied, and evil walks free, the universe seeks balance in strange and mysterious ways. Not all rebirths are for peace—some are born for reckoning.

And thus, where her story ended, another began.

A cry reborn.

A vow unfulfilled.

A boy named Shiv.

And the fire of a soul that refused to forget.

Because sometimes, the only way justice arrives... is through **REINCARNATION**.

The Night She Was Silenced

The narrow alley was dark, and the air thick with an unsettling stillness. Sati quickened her pace. She had stayed later than intended at her pregnant aunt's house, and now the village clock had struck ten. The night was heavy, its silence broken only by the rustling leaves and distant cries of a lone dog. A sense of dread gripped her; the shortcut through the alley seemed like the quickest way home, but something in her gut told her to turn back.

Suddenly, four figures materialized in the shadows—Tarak, Tripur, Bhasma, and Kami. Their faces were obscured by the night, but their eyes gleamed with a malevolent hunger.

"Where are you going in such a hurry, beautiful?" Tarak sneered, his lips curling into a wicked smile. "The night is still young."

Sati's heart pounded in her chest, but she managed to keep her voice steady. "Move aside," she demanded, "Let me pass."

Tripur laughed, a chilling, guttural sound that sent shivers down her spine. "Why the rush, darling? How about we accompany you?"

Fear and rage coursed through her veins in equal measure. She turned on her heel, ready to flee, but before she could take a step, they closed in around her like a pack of wolves. Her screams ripped through the night, but the village remained asleep, oblivious to her cries. Within moments, it was over. Sati's breath faltered, her body collapsed to the ground, and her eyes—wide with pain and fury—stared unseeing at the starless sky above.

The village awoke the next morning to a collective gasp of horror. Sati's murder sent ripples of shock through the tight-knit community. The police dismissed it as yet another tragic statistic, closing the case without a single arrest. Her death became another grim story told in hushed tones, a wound that festered with every passing day.

Yet, the gods seemed to have other plans.

CHAPTER TWO

Ashes Don't Forget

A few days after Sati's funeral, her aunt gave birth to a son. The villagers murmured about fate's strange play, whispering of karmic circles and divine retribution. The boy was named Shiv. From the moment he opened his eyes, there was something different about him—an inexplicable depth, as though he carried the weight of lifetimes. His mother noticed it first, the way he would gaze into the distance, as if remembering something far beyond his years.

Shiv was no ordinary child. As he grew up, he seemed to know things that no one had ever taught him. He became fiercely protective of the women in the village, and by the time he was a young man, he had taken up the humble job of an auto-rickshaw driver near the local girls' college. But Shiv did more than just drive; he taught the girls self-defense techniques, advising them on how to stay safe. His presence became a comforting shadow, a silent guardian watching over them.

One day, as Shiv stood with his friend Nandu, a small crowd of girls gathered around him. He was demonstrating the use of pepper spray. "Never walk alone at night," he warned, "And always keep this with you."

Nandu snickered, "Bro, you spend all day giving free advice to the girls. Can't you see I've been standing here waiting for some attention too?"

Shiv laughed, "What's the problem now, Nandu?"

"It's Suyasha," Nandu sighed. "She hasn't replied to my messages for three days."

"Maybe because she's tired of your daily drama," Shiv teased.

Eventually, Shiv gave in to Nandu's pleading and agreed to accompany him to Suyasha's house. When they arrived, Suyasha slammed the door in their faces. Shiv knocked persistently until she finally opened it, looking annoyed.

"Shiv, tell this idiot to bring me some chocolates," she demanded, "Or I'm done with him."

With a grin, Shiv returned to Nandu. "Just buy her the chocolates, man. She'll be fine in two minutes."

The two friends chuckled, bought the chocolates, and delivered them, leaving Suyasha appeased, for the time being.

CHAPTER THREE

The Auto Avenger

Days later, Shiv's life took a new turn. While passing the Vishnu temple, he saw a girl, Shakti, praying with serene intensity. As she exited the temple, a group of thugs cornered her. One of them leered, "Looking quite colorful today, aren't we?"

Though fear flickered in her eyes, Shakti maintained a calm front. "Let me go. What do you want?"

Shiv, sensing danger, wasted no time. "Get lost," he growled, "Or I'll make sure you regret the day you were born."

The leader of the gang sneered, "Who do you think you are?"

Without warning, Shiv's fist shot out, striking the man square in the jaw. The thug staggered and fell, clutching his face. "If you don't leave now, no one will be left to count your bones," Shiv threatened.

Seeing their leader down, the others hesitated, then bolted. Shakti exhaled, relief washing over her face. "Thank you," she said, "You saved me. Who are you?"

Shiv smiled, "I'm Shiv. I drive an auto around here. Let me take you home."

And so it began—a routine of daily meetings at the temple, conversations that stretched long into the evenings, laughter that felt like music to their ears. It didn't take long for love to bloom, and soon enough, they were married, with the blessings of their families.

CHAPTER FOUR

Fists, Faith & Fire

Yet, even the newfound joy of marriage could not soothe the restlessness in Shiv's heart. One night, as he stared out into the darkness, Shakti came up behind him, placing a gentle hand on his shoulder. "Shiv," she asked softly, "Are you hiding something from me? Tell me the truth."

Shiv turned to face her, his expression grave. "Yes," he whispered. "There is something I've never told anyone. I am... I am Sati."

Shakti's eyes widened with shock, disbelief mingling with tears. "Sati? The girl who was murdered twenty-five years ago? How...? How is this possible?"

Shiv's voice trembled as he spoke, "It wasn't just murder—it was rape and murder. I was reborn as Shiv to avenge my death, to ensure no woman in this village ever suffers the same fate again."

Shakti took a deep breath, her resolve hardening. "Then this fight is ours now, Shiv. I stand with you."

And so, Shiv was no longer alone.

CHAPTER FIVE

The Final Name

With Nandu's help, Shiv had already dealt with three of the four men—Tarak, Tripur, and Bhasma. Only Kami remained.

Shiv set a trap, luring Kami to an old, abandoned Shiva temple on the outskirts of the village. The temple was shrouded in darkness, the air thick with a sense of foreboding.

Kami's voice trembled as he shouted into the void, "Who are you? Why are you doing this? Let me go!"

From the shadows, Shiv's voice emerged, deep and haunting, repeating Tripur's taunting words from that fateful night, "Why the rush, darling? How about we accompany you?"

Kami's face drained of color as the memory of that night resurfaced, a night that had come back to haunt him. In a desperate attempt, Kami lunged at Shiv, but his attack was clumsy, driven by fear. Shiv deflected the blow, sending Kami sprawling into an ancient fire pit.

Nandu arrived just in time, tossing a gun to Shiv. But Kami had grabbed a weapon of his own. They fired simultaneously. Both men collapsed, mortally wounded. As Kami gasped for breath, Shiv whispered, "After tonight, no one like you will ever be born in this village again."

Kami's body hit the ground with a final thud, and Shiv felt his life slipping away. Nandu and Shakti rushed to his side, but they were too late. Shiv's eyes fluttered shut, his spirit leaving his body.

At that moment, Shiv's mother arrived, her face etched with grief. A brilliant light emerged from Shiv's lifeless form—a divine glow from the deity Ardhanarishvara, merging into the ancient Shivling at the temple's center. As dawn broke, the darkness dissipated, replaced by a new light.

CHAPTER SIX

Where Gods Reside

The next day, the entire village gathered at the temple. A divine voice echoed from the heavens:

Where women are honored, there the gods reside
Where they are not, all actions remain fruitless

And with that, the story of Sati's rebirth and Shiv's vengeance came full circle, a tale that would be told for generations to come.